ONCE UPON A FABLE

*"I long for scenes where man has never trod
A place where woman never smiled or wept;
There to abide with my creator, God,
And sleep as I in childhood sweetly slept,*

. . . .

from John Clare, "I Am!"

Books by Mariah Robinson

Love and Other Illusions
Sister Sorrow, Sister Joy

ONCE UPON A FABLE

Mariah Robinson

Brandylane Publishers, Inc.
Publishing books since 1985

Jefferson Madison
Regional Library
Charlottesville, Virginia

Copyright 2020 by Mariah Robinson.

No part of this book may be reproduced in any form or by any electronic or mechanical means, or the facilitation thereof, including information storage and retrieval systems, without permission in writing from the publisher, except in the case of brief quotations published in articles and reviews. Any educational institution wishing to photocopy part or all of the work for classroom use, or individual researchers who would like to obtain permission to reprint the work for educational purposes, should contact the publisher.

Credit:
"Anything will give up its secrets if you love it enough."
—George Washington Carver, pg. 63

"We look before and after, / And pine for what is not . . . / Our sweetest songs are those that tell of saddest thought"
—from "To a Skylark" by Percy Bysshe Shelley, pg. 76

"He prayeth best, who loveth best / all things both great and small"
—from "The Rime of the Ancient Mariner" by William Taylor Coleridge, pg.76

"Such men as he be never at heart's ease / Whiles they behold a greater than themselves, / And therefore are they very dangerous"
—from "Julius Caesar" by William Shakespeare, pg. 76

Cover image: *The Ass and the Little Dog* by Jean de La Fontaine

ISBN: 978-1-947860-19-3
LCCN: 2020901452

Printed in the United States

Published by Brandylane Publishers, Inc.
5 S. 1st Street
Richmond, Virginia 23219
brandylanepublishers.com | belleislebooks.com

For my mother

*"Forget your perfect offering.
Everything has a crack in it. Everything.
That's how the Light gets in."*

—*Leonard Cohen, Anthem*

And for my father

"Trust in Allah and tie your camel to the post."
—*Ancient Sufi proverb*

This is a work of fiction. Names, characters, businesses, places, events, locales, and incidents are either the products of the author's imagination or used in a fictitious manner. Any resemblance to actual persons, living or dead, or actual events is purely coincidental.

*"Too much reality is **NOT** what the people want."*
—Stardust Memories

FABLES

Leave Her to Heaven
1

A Raven Named Rubin
19

The Beginning of Wisdom
27

Mayor Spare That Tree
39

Bridge in the Afternoon
55

The Good the Bad and the Hideous
71

There's No Business Like Show Business
87

LEAVE HER TO HEAVEN

For Mabel and Ruby

*"Nothing is more profound than
what appears on the surface."*
—**Hegel**

Sasha Goforth was a purebred Siamese, with brilliant sapphire eyes boldly set in a finely chiseled head. Her mask, ears, tail, and paws were ebony, and she had a lithe, Lauren Bacall body and yowl. She first met Jay Williamson, a grey-and-white striped tabby with six toes on his left front paw, large hazel eyes, and a lazy Cheshire cat grin that belied the complexity of his inner world, at a Fleetwood Mac concert, in Winston Salem, North Carolina. They fell in love, married two weeks after the concert, made a down payment on a condo in Durham, and, after Jay had completed his residency in oral surgery, they bought a vintage pre-Civil War farmhouse on the outskirts of Biloxi, Mississippi. The sale of the Durham condo covered the down payment, the re-plastering, rewiring, painting, air conditioning, and the sanding and sealing of the random width, heart-of-pine floors.

They moved in as soon as the freshly painted walls and ceilings would allow, and Jay began his practice in a long-vacated High's ice cream parlor on Main Street, and Sasha began editing manuscripts for an offbeat Manhattan publishing house.

The Williamsons were now well into the third year of marriage, but the union lacked the harmony with which it had begun. For reasons never fully diagnosed, Sasha, who had gotten pregnant thirteen times, was never able to carry her litters to term. That and Jay's steadily declining dental practice seemed the most ostensible causes of their discontent. They consulted a Freudian psychotherapist who diagnosed and wrote a monthly column for the Ladies Home Journal, entitled "Can This Marriage Be Saved?" The therapist advised Sasha to consider adoption and cautioned Jay against being too casual with female patients during root canals.

Sasha was in the kitchen eating a sardine sandwich when the front door opened, and in walked Jay. It was one o'clock in the afternoon, and he never came home that early.

"We have a problem," he informed her. "A serious problem."

Sasha swallowed a chunk of inadequately chewed sardine. "What's the problem?"

"I've gotten a Burmese pregnant," he answered without preamble, "and she's not going to have the litter aborted, and she's not going to rear them either. It appears that rearing them is to going to be my responsibility."

Sasha's eyes narrowed. "Who is she?"

"An unspectacular hygienist hussy from Doug Brayer's office," he replied. "I never gave her a second glance before or since that appointment," he scowled. "I was going to reschedule because Doug had gone home sick, and the rest of the staff took off after Doug left and I would have left, too, but for that Burmese tramp who . . . who . . . well . . . she locked the office door behind the receptionist, and then she ditched her uniform jacket, replaced the piped-in music with a sultry Nina Simone CD, and slapped a mask filled with laughing gas over my nostrils—which I never should have inhaled but did inhale and, after which . . ."

He scratched his chin with his sixth toe. "After which everything went straight to hell in a handbag," he confessed.

He shook his head from side to side—an escalating succession of guilt-laden acknowledgments. "Those snaps on that skimpy white uniform of hers kept popping open," he recounted, "and she wanted me to snap them closed because...well...well because she couldn't seem to manage them by herself, and because she had to re-take my X-rays three or four times because she couldn't seem to manage them by herself either." His ears reddened, and his whiskers began to twitch. "Every time she bent over me, those snaps would pop open and out would pop her...her..." His throat tightened, and he reverted to silence and then went to the fridge and poured out a bowlful of half and half, which he rapidly lapped down.

"The X-rays she took were completely unreadable," he rasped, "and although she insisted she had thoroughly cleaned my teeth, I was not asked even once to rinse and spit. I was asked to pay, mind you, to pay the bill as if...as if my once-yearly check-up had been professionally handled and completed, which was most certainly not the case."

His ears turned a more purplish red, and his jaw muscles began to pulsate. "I swear, Sasha, it never happened except that one time, and it will never happen again." He pressed his abundantly whiskered jowl against Sasha's elegant muzzle. "I'm sorry, Honey. Please say you'll forgive me."

Sasha pushed him away and stalked out of the kitchen, into the hallway and upstairs to the spacious and tall-ceilinged sitting room where she proofed manuscripts. She closed the door behind her and sat at her desk. Then, with a furious sweep of paw, she sent the entire desktop crashing to the floor and burst into tears.

Two weeks later, the Burmese gave birth. Jay brought the litter home in a brown paper lunch bag and deposited it unceremoniously on the hall table.

"Premature," he informed Sasha, "and it's hard to decide which of them is the homeliest. Lord, what a misbegotten threesome. Just take them to The Biloxi Homeless Society Shelter. They'll know what to do for them. I have a two o'clock emergency extraction, for which I'm already forty minutes late."

Sasha called the shelter for directions and was informed that they closed at noon on Wednesdays and that she could bring them in tomorrow morning. She went down to the basement and returned to her ironing, but she couldn't concentrate on her work, and she scorched the collar of Jay's favorite pink oxford cloth shirt. Something dark and anxiety-laden impelled her back upstairs, into the hallway, and over to the oak library table on which the brown bag with the twisted neck had been left. "Hell and damnation," she said in a strangled whisper, "I'll just drown them in the kitchen sink and end their misbegotten little lives now—the hell with tomorrow morning."

She filled the sink with tepid water, strode into the hallway, snatched the bag from the library table and headed back to the kitchen. The bag had surprising heft, so she held it away from her body with her right paw and put her left paw under it to support its weight.

She could feel the warmth of living flesh through the thin brown paper, and she could discern the sound of faintly scratching claws. She sat down at the kitchen table, placed the bag on her lap, and opened it cautiously, and when she saw the newborn kits with their bitten-off umbilical cords and their tiny wobbling heads on their tiny wobbling necks, her heart split like an overripe watermelon and overflowed like the Biloxi River at high tide.

Jay came home that evening to a kitchen that reeked of Similac. He spied the three tiny baby doll bottles, and on the kitchen table lay Sasha's knitting basket filled with scraps of rags and twists of cotton yarn and his favorite pink shirt, minus the button-hole strip, the buttons, the cuffs, and a badly scorched collar.

Sasha had the three mewling kits on her lap, and her face looked young and peaceful and soft—softer than he could ever remember it looking.

"Don't you go falling in love," he warned, "because we're not keeping them."

"You just go to hell," she retorted and returned her love-filled gaze to the babes on her lap. "You just go straight to hell in a handbag, and take that unspectacular Burmese hussy tooth cleaner with you. And forget supper. I'm not cooking tonight."

Within two weeks, the kits' cords dried up and disappeared, their eyes opened, and soft silken fur covered the rounded crowns of their skulls. The female kit had black fur that gave off mahogany glints in sunlight and round emerald eyes without even a hint of brown or yellow. The two male kits were identical and looked Burmese, except for their paws, which were cream colored. They were all beautiful. The males were more easy-going than the female, who swiped at her brothers whenever they came near her, and who, when she nursed from the bottle, would drool saliva down her chin and onto Sasha's lap, leaving circles of damp.

Sasha named the boys Curtis and Charlie and the girl Blanche, from the Tennessee Williams play A Streetcar Named Desire.

Their friends congratulated Jay and Sasha and said that the babies were precious, that the boys looked just like Sasha, and that Blanche would grow up to be a heartbreaker. Jay was too abashed to say anything except "Thank you," and Sasha accepted the compliments with equanimity. What did it matter how and with whom? She and Jay were their mom and dad now, she was content to raise them as their own, and Jay had heard that the Burmese hussy had gone and gotten herself pregnant again and had married the father, a part-Persian guitarist from Nashville, where they were now living with their newborn litter of three.

The years passed. Curtis graduated from high school, moved to New York, became a beautician, and took up residence with a Portuguese born-and-bred electrician named Garcia, who had bought and was currently restoring a huge old Brooklyn brownstone with tall ceilings and fourteen fireplaces.

Charlie, the most studious of the three, decided he wanted to become a lawyer. He graduated from Duke with honors, attended Washington and Lee law school, graduated top of his class, and set up practice in Jacksonville, Florida. Shortly thereafter, he fell in love with and married a Siamese beauty named Ursula. They had twin daughters, plenty of money, lived in a good neighborhood, and were content. The twins were sweet natured and loved to visit Jay and Sasha. They all came regularly for Christmas and Thanksgiving, and the twins spent two weeks with Jay and Sasha every summer.

Blanche joined the Peace Corps after graduating from UNC, but quit after three months of grueling fieldwork in Nairobi. "My nerves just couldn't take it," she wept. She then took a seminar in macrobiotics but gave it up because the food caused her continuously to belch and she began losing fur. Her father managed to get her into dental school, but she dropped out after a year because the incessant high-pitched whine of the drill initiated agonizing migraines that incapacitated her for days on end. She became addicted to the Demerol she took for the pain, and her father financed six months in the Sonoran Desert Rehabilitative Haven for the Spiritually Disenfranchised. During one of several consciousness-raising private sessions, she became pregnant by the Haven's recently appointed and reputedly brilliant Jungian psychoanalyst who had four young children but was unhappily married. The pregnancy caused crippling and ceaseless bouts of nausea and vomiting. She had an abortion, which caused crippling and ceaseless bouts of guilt-laden irritable bowel syndrome, for which she took a form of organically cultivated belladonna that put an end to the syndrome but gave rise to a severe yeast infection. After months of every holistic treatment known to man, she had a tubal ligation. The ligation put an end to the yeast infection but caused bloating and debilitating mood swings. Her gynecologist prescribed Prozac, which eliminated the mood swings, but elicited serious weight gain. She then charged to her dad and hired two construction workers to securely pitch—a sizeable, no-expense-spared tent—in the Arizona desert sands, where she spent three months fasting and praying. The fasting took care of the weight gain, but she acquired an itchy, angry, and rapidly spreading rash from tiny sand crabs that had somehow infiltrated her lush, air-filled sleeping bag. A Tucson Valley emergency room doctor agreed to Blanche's request for a strong dose of steroids, which quickly cleared up the rash and eliminated the itching but brought on rapid mood swings and a secondary rash.

Blanche mainly relayed these events to Jay and Sasha by telephone. She seldom came home and when she did, she spent most of her visit with friends.

Curtis called home often. He and Garcia were doing great, but Garcia had been diagnosed HIV positive, and the medicine was horribly expensive and caused unpleasant side effects. Sasha worried that Curtis might catch the virus, but Curtis assured his mother that he was tested regularly and that he and Garcia were mindful and that they would be down for a long visit soon.

The years continued to accumulate. Jay achieved a solid practice, Sasha was made senior editor, and their combined incomes made it possible to restore the old farmhouse, add a swimming pool, cultivate a vegetable garden, and rebuild and modernize the greenhouse with high-tech heating, cooling, and irrigation systems.

They had good children, considerate and loyal friends, peaceful neighbors, two lovely teenage granddaughters, and their marriage had survived intact.

It felt to Sasha as if the summer months grew longer and the winter days and nights grew brief of duration, but Jay said 'not so'—that the passage of time was as it had always been and that she remained as girlishly timeless as she was when he first saw her wearing that pink and green madras jumpsuit, and those evasive movie-star sunglasses, at that awesome Fleetwood Mac concert.

Early one chilly March morning, just after Jay had left for work, there was a knock at the door, and in walked Blanche. Her face was hard and cold. "I had a DNA test," she blurted, "and I don't have a drop of Siamese blood in me. Am I adopted?"

"No, you're not adopted," Sasha replied. "Well, yes, I guess you are adopted. Well, yes and no."

"You guess? Yes and no?" Blanche's eyes slitted. "What the hell does that mean?"

"It means that you are Jay's natural child but that I am not your birth mother."

And then Sasha shared what she knew of Blanche's birth mother. She flinched at the disdain in Blanche's eyes, but she bore the girl's loathing stoically. And when Blanche stormed out, slamming the heavy oak front door so furiously that the parlor windows shook, Sasha walked tiredly upstairs to her study, put her head in her paws and wept.

Sasha waited until after supper to tell Jay what had happened.

"You did the right thing," he said and enfolded her in his arms. "You did the right thing. That girl has never cared about you." His voice roughened. "She's been like that from day one. I could see it in the way she looked at you when you fed her and cleaned her. The way she talked to you. The way she talked about you. The way she never thanked you much for anything, never helped you much with anything."

He gazed into Sasha's eyes. They were the eyes of a felled calf, and Jay remembered the Christmas Sasha had bought matching sweaters for Blanche and herself. They were from the Peruvian Kitty Cat Connection, and they were classy and pricey.

"Try yours on," Sasha had suggested. "If you like it, I'll wear mine, too."

"Forget it," Blanche had retorted. "I'm so not into mother-daughter articles of clothing." She had deposited the sweater back into its box and shoved the box beneath the Christmas tree and when she left for San Francisco the following morning, the sweater had not accompanied her.

Jay stroked Sasha's cheek. "I'm sorry, honey, but there it is. I saw it, and you never saw it, but there it is."

"But why doesn't Blanche care about me?" Sasha pleaded and her eyes searched his countenance for the answer.

"I don't know why," Jay replied after a long silence. "The answers to most of the why's of life elude me and this one's no exception."

He emitted a slow growl, captured Sasha's chin

with his sixth toe, and nipped the tips of her pointy black ears with his pointy white teeth. "I haven't a clue as to why our daughter is disloyal to and disrespectful of her mother..." He softly nipped Sasha's sleek throat, "I only know that she is."

Months passed. Sasha and Jay didn't discuss Blanche again but, for some unclear reason, instead of being a bone of contention between them, it brought them closer together. Jay was loving and kind to her in ways that he had never before been. He brought her flowers and closed his practice for two weeks and took her to New York to visit Curtis and Garcia. They stayed at the Plaza, spent afternoons at the Metropolitan, the Guggenheim, and the Frick museums, took Curtis and Garcia to dinner at the Four Seasons and Lutéce and Sunday brunch at Tavern on the Green, strolled endlessly through Central Park, window-shopped at the best of the best, browsed renowned antique galleries and high end art galleries, and attended three Broadway plays.

And then they flew to Jacksonville and spent a week with Charlie and Ursula and the granddaughters. They laughed, teased, nuzzled and snuggled together, drank well-aged cognac and watched vintage movies in the spacious guest suite of Curtis and Ursula's fine house, and fell in love all over again.

Sasha was preparing freshly-picked-from-the-garden okra when Jay walked into the kitchen. She glanced at the clock. It was three-thirty. "You're home early," she said.

"I cancelled my last appointment. Blanche called me at the office this afternoon. She had called a couple of weeks ago and informed my secretary that I was to send a gob of saliva, in an airtight vial, UPS, overnight delivery, for DNA testing, which I did, and the results of which strongly suggest that I am not Blanche's biological father."

Sasha's jaw dropped. "How could that be possible?"

"It could be possible," he replied, grim of voice. "If that Burmese hussy was already pregnant by some other tomcat and pinned it on me. I seem to recall that those kittens came a lot earlier than they should have, given the date of my yearly oral exam."

Sasha recalled the sheen of Blanche's luxuriant ebony fur in the sunlight—the pure green of her eyes, the pliant softness of her body. "A black, part Persian musician other tomcat," she growled, and her brow furrowed in rapidly dawning comprehension. "I ought to have been more cautious about taking those helpless critters on," her voice softened, "but I fell in love the second I looked into that bag. I never thought it through. I just fell in love." An image of the tiny bobbing heads flashed, and her heart clenched. She exhaled a sigh. "What else did Blanche say?"

"She said that she's joined an Adoption Anonymous group and that they are going to help her find her real parents and that she is so totally over you as her mother and . . ." He swallowed hard. "And now me, as her dad."

Sasha endured the second clench of heart. She pondered what she and Jay would say to their sons and how their sons would feel about it. One thing they would never be told about was the squirming lunch bag with its twisted neck, resting on the library table in the hallway—that was for sure.

"Well," she said to her husband, "you and I can manage to live serenely together, despite Blanche's being so over us, can't we?"

She witnessed Jay's dazed grief, and her eyes filled and her ears flattened. She went to him, stroked his muzzle, smoothed his disheveled fur, and kissed his gray-whiskered cheek.

"Don't do this to yourself, my love," she gently cautioned. "Suffering over this is painful, pointless, and definitely no longer the way to go. Blanche maintains a seriously self-serving consciousness, bulwarked by a seriously self-absorbed ego. It's how she copes with the rigors of a seriously self-centered existence, and it's true of practically everyone who lives and breathes on planet Earth."

She scratched Jay's ears and nuzzled his broad rosy nose with her narrow ebony nose until he began to purr.

"We never stressed gratitude from our children," she reflected. "We have friends who did with their offspring . . . and probably still do . . . only we never did and probably never will." Her face settled into impassive neutrality. "But that's all beside the point because Blanche is middle-aged now, and she's beautiful and educated, has perfect teeth, and lives a merciful three thousand miles away. Circumstances may not have been what we believed they were, but I'm glad we didn't put the facts together back then, because we would have done differently for sure. Or . . ." She stopped to ponder the mystical and possibility-laden notion that had just occurred to her. "Perhaps," she mused, "in accordance with a divine plan—a divine plan entirely unknown to us—it was decided ... it was destined for Blanche and Curtis and Charlie to be raised as our own."

Time fell away and Sasha relived her first encounter with the trio of newborns—trembling—blind—completely helpless.

And then time returned her to the three of them as they were now. Middle-aged. Competent. Attractive.

"Blanche and Charlie and Curtis are our experience of raising children." She reflected. "We can never know how our world would have turned without them at the center of it precisely because there they were at the center of it. It's that simple and that profound."

She gave Jay's neck another tender nuzzle, and then she walked over to the stove, turned up the flame, dropped the battered okra, piece by piece, into the rapidly boiling oil, and began setting the kitchen table for their supper.

"First—Chill—then stupor—then the letting go."
Emily Dickinson,
"After great pain a formal feeling comes"

A RAVEN NAMED RUBIN

For Auntie Del

"I give you for courage
A light heart that sings,
And I who have never flown
Give you my wings."

—Emma Gray Trigg,
A Mother To Her Daughter

Sally and Della were returning from the garden when Della spied the raven. At first, she thought it was a black rock, but when she looked more closely she saw the downy head and tightly furled pinfeathers. "Look!" she whispered to Sally and pointed at the motionless bird.

"Why, it's a very young raven!" Sally exclaimed.

"Is it alive?" Della asked.

"Yes, I think it is," Sally answered, "so be careful."

Della circled the bird cautiously. It did not move, but its eyes opened when she lightly touched its wing.

"What should we do?" she asked her sister.

"We can't do anything by ourselves. We'll have to get help." Sally looked up at the chestnut tree above the bird. "There's a nest way up there. You can barely see it. It might have fallen from that nest. But it's strange that there aren't any ravens around to watch over it. Ravens are very protective of their offspring."

Della took four green peas and half a dozen kernels of fresh corn from her beaded reticule. "Maybe it's hungry," she said.

"It probably needs water," Sally said. "I don't think it's at all well. Why don't you stay here with it, and I'll go for help."

Della placed the vegetables back in her reticule and handed it to Sally. "Here, you take these vegetables home to Mama. She's making a stew for our supper tonight."

When Sally left, Della seated herself alongside the quiet bird. "Don't worry," she said to the raven in her most reassuring voice. "You're going to be fine. Sally will find someone to help you."

The raven remained silent, but its soft, small bird body seemed to settle itself into Della's equally soft and small field mouse body. Della tried to stay awake and watchful, but she was exhausted from foraging in cook's garden and she fell asleep within minutes.

It was the gloaming of the evening when Della awakened to the sound of high-pitched chattering.

Sally and seven of their siblings were dragging a pallet of cornhusks laced together with straw.

The raven's eyes were open and watchful, but it remained motionless.

Gus, the firstborn of their litter, gave brief instructions. The pallet was to be placed right next to the raven's body. They would slide the bird's body onto the husks, and then the mice would slide their bodies gently under the pallet and carefully transport it to the barn. Sally and Della were to walk alongside the pallet to make sure the bird stayed put.

Della whispered reassuringly to the raven throughout the slow trek to the barn. She was concerned that the bird might be frightened or try to get away, but it closed its eyes and never moved a muscle or made even a tiny awk of protest.

When they finally reached the barn, Mama was waiting. She ran her front paws expertly over the bird's body. "Nothing seems out of place," she said. She placed her nose to the bird's beak. "Its breathing is shallow," she told them. "The only thing to do is to give it some water and see what the morning brings."

Gus dipped an empty pea pod into a cistern of rainwater and handed it to his mother, who stroked the bird's throat, tapped the side of its pointed black beak, and, when the beak opened, fed it water, drop by patient drop. She nodded approval when she saw that the bird was swallowing the droplets. "That's a good sign. Now let's carry it over to that old wooden birdcage, where it will be safe for the night."

She urged her offspring into the small mouse hole in the barn's rear wall. "C'mon now, you must all be hungry for your supper."

But Della would not be persuaded to leave the raven alone. She climbed into the cage with it. "I want to stay the night with it, Mama," she pleaded. "It will surely be frightened if we leave it by itself."

Mama gave Della the piece of freshly baked cornbread she had in her apron pocket. "I had intended it for the bird, but it's much too weak to eat anything," she told Della. "You can have it for your supper."

Della ate hungrily, leaving a few morsels in case the raven got hungry. Then she cleaned her whiskers and paws and said her evening prayers. She said a special prayer for the baby raven. She prayed that God would watch over it during the night, and then she settled herself between the raven's legs and fell asleep.

She dreamed of the raven. She dreamed that its name was Rubin and that he was all well and grown-up, with beautiful black wings that propelled him out of the barn and into the glorious sunlit sky, and that she was riding with Rubin on his broad shiny black tail, and that she didn't even have to hold on to keep from falling. She dreamed that she and Rubin were soaring—soaring—soaring—and they were happy—happy—happy.

She dreamed and awakened ecstatic. She was surprised to find she was still in the cage, still nestled between the bird's tiny legs and claws. She tilted her head sideways and gazed into its wide-open eyes. "I dreamed that you were flying," she whispered, "that you were carrying me on your tail, and that your name was Rubin, and you and I were the best of friends. Promise me that when you get well and have learned to fly, you will take me up into the sky with you."

The raven's eyes filled with a brilliantly glowing inner light. He held onto Della with his matchstick legs and tightened them slowly, ever so slowly, around her body and then he lifted his head up to the heavens and emitted a single powerful croak that resonated throughout the high rafters of the barn. He held Della even more tightly for a very long moment, and then he exhaled a brief sigh and his claws slowly loosened their hold, and Della knew that Rubin was to be no more and she wept.

They buried him in the morning, under the old chestnut tree where Della had first spied him. Gus recited the prayer for the dead and Della and Sally placed two tender white daisies atop the grave they had fashioned for Rubin.

After the service was ended and they were returning to the barn, Della looked back and saw overhead, a ceremony of ravens, gliding above the gravesite in a slow arc of tribute.

"Ah! Surely nothing dies but something mourns."
George Gordon, Lord Byron

THE BEGINNING OF WISDOM

For my grandmother
"Can one commit a sin against an animal?
Oh yes. One can commit a sin against a blade of grass. "
—*Orca*

It was a sunlit, late spring afternoon.

Nanny was having tea with Cook, and Gabriel Ashworth was searching the flowering trees in his grandfather's orchard for insects to capture and put in the jar he had brought along. He had lined the glass bottom with fresh grass, and his grandfather's gardener had made holes in the metal cap. He already had collected a pair of inchworms, an orange-and-black spotted beetle, and a dozen or so tiny rust-colored ants on a partially nibbled mulberry leaf. He was eyeing a fat horned snail that was slowly wending its way up an apple-laden tree branch when he saw the squirrel, watching him watch the snail.

The squirrel was striking of appearance. His fur coat, glinting in the sunlight, was many-colored. His eyes were black, shiny, and unafraid.

And his tail!

His tail was amazing!

"Why, good afternoon, you wonderful squirrel!" Gabriel exclaimed. "Do you have a name?"

The squirrel ignored the question and looked pointedly at the glass jar Gabriel was holding. "Where are you taking Libby?"

Gabriel peered into the jar. "Which one's Libby?"

"She has a red shell with black spots and she's laid baby ladybug eggs—many baby ladybug eggs."

"How many eggs has she laid and how do you know that?" Gabriel asked.

"Libby and I live in the same tree," The squirrel replied. "Libby has a family of sorts." He extended his tail in a slow twirl. "Everything does."

Gabriel stared at the squirrel. "Everything does what?"

"Everything has a family of sorts."

"Do you have a family of sorts?"

"Indeed," the squirrel replied matter-of-factly. He pricked his tiny ears and peered beyond Gabriel. "Your nanny is coming. Perhaps you should set those captured insects free before she catches up with you. She'll empty the jar and crush them with the heel of her shoe, as she did last week."

He gave his tail another, more rapid twirl and scampered to a taller branch and then to another and then another.

"Please," Gabriel called after him. "Won't you tell me your name?"

"I'm Joseph Bottomley," the squirrel called down and then he disappeared from sight.

⁕

"What do you have in that jar, Gabriel?" Nanny asked. She was panting from the hot tea, the brisk walk, her tight shoes and corset, and the warm day, all of which made her face look red, pinched, and stony.

Gabriel crossed the index and middle fingers of his right hand before telling the fib. "It's an angry buzzing wasp, Nanny, so you'd best move away while I set it free." He quickly unscrewed the jar's lid and tossed its contents.

Nanny hurried away. "Don't linger, Gabriel. That was a foolish thing to do. That wasp might sting you for having captured it. Wasps are vindictive."

"Yes, Nanny," Gabriel replied. He screwed the lid

back on the jar and caught up with her. "She could have stung me," he reflected "but she was worrying about the babies she's going to have."

"And how, pray tell, did you come to know that the wasp was a she and that she was going to have babies, Gabriel?"

"I know because a squirrel told me."

"A squirrel told you, Gabriel? A talking squirrel shared a confidence concerning a female wasp with you? How do you come up with such nonsense?" Nanny remonstrated and took the jar from his hand. "You mustn't run with a glass jar in your hand, Gabriel. You could easily trip, crash the glass, and lose an eye. Dreadful things befall little boys and girls who disregard their nannies' warnings."

Gabriel's right eye squinched shut. He could feel the accident, not as if it were just now happening, but as if it had already happened—as if he were already a pirate or a left-eyed Cyclops.

He held Nanny's hand more tightly. "I don't think I want to capture insects anymore, Nanny."

"Oh, I don't mind that part of it for you. Insects are excellent specimens to capture and dissect. How and why the good Lord came up with bugs in the first place, I can't begin to imagine. No, Gabriel, I'm pleased that you take an interest in nature. Perhaps you'll decide to become a physician like your grandfather when you grow up. Hurry now; you mustn't be late for supper."

Later that evening, after supper, his bath and Bible bedtime story from Nanny, and evening prayers with Mommy and Daddy, Gabriel lay in his trundle bed and recounted the events of his day.

He thought about his new afternoon acquaintance. He pondered how the squirrel might have come to be named Joseph Bottomley. Perhaps he was called "Joseph" because his tail and coat of thick fur, gleaming in the sunlight, gave off glints of red and orange and green and amber and shiny gold—like young Joseph's many colored coat that was stolen when Joseph was sold by his brothers into slavery... And he was pretty sure that "Bottomley" was the last name of Joseph's mom and dad.

He pondered how Joseph Bottomley knew that Libby was in the jar and if Joseph Bottomley knew the names of all of the captured insects in that jar. Why, there were at least a dozen ants on just that one leaf! And there was a pair of inchworms in there, too!

Gabriel tried to remember the many insects he had captured and put in containers and then stashed away in his closet and forgotten. He would come upon them, days and sometimes weeks later, their bodies shriveled up and lifeless—dead because he had neglected to provide them with air and food and water—dead because he had forgotten that they were trapped—unable to scurry back—hop back—fly back—to their homes and families of sorts—probably some of them with children waiting to be fed or with babies waiting to be born.

As he had waited until it was time for him to be born.

Gabriel wondered what became of bugs when they died. Where did they go? Did they have funerals like the one they'd had for his great-grandmother?

He sighed. It was the only time he had seen his

mother weep. Gabriel had asked his father, later that evening, after the house had emptied of family and friends and all of the funeral food and whiskey had been put away, what it felt like to die.

His father had thought for a long while. "I don't really know a thing about death, Gabriel," he had answered. "I do believe that death will be as amazing an adventure when it comes to each of us, as the adventure of our having been born. I can't think of any reason why it should be otherwise," he had reflected, smoothing Gabriel's tousled hair into a tidy side part with gentle fingers, "but it's very sad, Gabriel, particularly for your mother, that Nana is no longer able to be with us."

Gabriel had no memory of how he felt when he was born. Probably happy, although television babies usually howled at birth. He wondered if baby insects howled when they got born. Insects were a lot different from human beings, but they were also a lot like human beings in the way that . . . that . . . well . . . that there were tons of differences in the faces and bodies of human beings just as there were tons of differences in the faces and bodies of bugs.

Why, there were tons and tons and tons of differences in bugs!

Gabriel began to recount the various possibilities of color and shading and length and width and body shape of bugs.

He considered how their eyes were sometimes beady and sometimes prominent.

And he considered the numbers and angles of

their legs, and the way they maneuvered those legs to get around.

And how some had wings and could fly anywhere they wanted.

And how some could dig long, narrow tunnels in the rich, grass-covered soil of the croquet lawn.

He pondered the marshmallow softness of caterpillars and snails.

The shiny hardness of beetles.

The protective, shield-shaped gray shell of stinkbugs.

The constantly vibrating antennae of the pale green grasshoppers that hopped about in Cook's garden and nibbled away at the leaves of her prized cabbages and lettuces and worked their way through the fibrous and layered husks that protected the hidden tender kernels of sweet summer corn.

He thought about the buzzing bees that built their hives in the English ivy that covered the old brick walls of his grandfather's house, and of how they gathered pollen from the ivy's clustered white blossoms and mysteriously turned it into the rich amber honey he spooned onto his morning oatmeal.

He thought about the never-ending repetition of a centipede's swiftly moving feet.

And then he remembered the colored and patterned wings of the mounted butterflies in the old leather-bound collection in his grandfather's study, and, when he remembered those impaled gaily patterned beauties, something strange began to happen to Gabriel. It began to feel as if his thumb were getting large—larger than his entire hand—and then larger than his entire body—or was it that the rest of his body was getting very tiny?

As tiny as a butterfly.

As tiny as Tom Thumb.

Gosh, he thought, this must be what it feels like to be Tom Thumb!

The excitement was quickly washed away by a wave of fear. His eyes shuddered closed. What if...if somewhere beyond the sky—on a secret planet in a secret part of outer space—secret creatures existed that were smarter and more powerful than human beings? Gabriel squeezed his eyes more tightly shut but his worries continued to mount. And what if...what if those secret creatures were able to capture, with huge, unbreakable, long-handled nets, human beings? To capture and then imprison human beings in huge glass jars—and keep them in huge leather bound scrapbooks—to impale the tender, downy skin that covered human bodies—to pierce through the interior body parts beneath human skin—the muscles—the stomach—the lungs—the beating heart that pumped the crimson blood into the veins of mommies and daddies, grandfathers and grandmothers, sisters, nannies, cooks, gardeners, policemen, Sunday school teachers, bank tellers, salesladies, doctors, nurses, dentists, flower-shop owners, bakery-shop owners, candy shop owners, cowboys and Indians, tinkers, tailors, soldiers, sailors, rich men, poor men, beggar men, thieves—all types and sorts of human beings—captured and killed and then mounted onto huge pages in huge scrapbooks and then kept on huge shelves in huge libraries— just like the dozens of butterflies his grandfather had caught with long-handled nets and now kept in that leather bound and monogrammed album in his study.

Was it possible, Gabriel fretted in growing misery, that those butterflies had been terrified inside their long-handled prisons of net? And what in the world had possessed Grandfather to capture those beautiful and harmless and totally helpless creatures, in the first place? Was it because they were so beautiful and rare and delicate, like his mother and sister and his sister's best friend, Eliza, who had long hair the color of buttercups and pink cheeks that rounded and dimpled when she laughed and who chased him until she caught up with him and then tickled him until he shrieked with laughter and pleaded for mercy?

A clutch of even greater panic took hold of Gabriel. Had those tiny and delicate butterflies suffered when Grandfather, with thumb and forefinger, stopped the flow of air into their ever-so-small thoraxes and . . . and how exactly had stopping that flow of air ended the life that had, only seconds before, vibrated inside their bodies and propelled their tissue-thin fluttery wings into the magic of flight?

Gabriel rolled onto his side and curled into a tightly protective sliver of crescent moon. He hated to think about pain, and he hated to think about dying. He hated pain and he was afraid to die.

He took a deep breath, exhaled, and then nodded his head in comprehension.

That was it, then.

He would never again capture bugs and put them in jars—not even the summertime fireflies he so liked to watch flicker off and on, inside their prisons of metal-capped glass. He had lots of reasons why he wasn't going to, but those reasons would be private between himself and his new good friend, Joseph Bottomley Squirrel.

He took another deep breath, whispered the promise, crossed his heart, and solemnly swore that he hoped to die if he broke that promise.

He was just rounding the corner to sleep when he decided that tomorrow, after he returned from school, he would ask Nanny if he could spend time in Grandfather's orchard while Nanny was having tea with Cook.

Perhaps he would find Joseph Bottomley climbing the branches of that very same apple tree.

And perhaps Libby's babies would have already been born.

And perhaps Joseph Bottomley would know just how many and what names Libby had chosen for each of them.

> "I will be the gladdest thing
> Under the sun!
> I will touch a hundred flowers
> And not pick one."
>
> Edna St. Vincent Millay
> *"Afternoon on a Hill"*

MAYOR SPARE THAT TREE

For Leake Wornom and Jack Pearsall

"Never hate your enemies.
It affects your judgment."
—*The Godfather Part II*

Liam Wilton was a rangy, soft-spoken raccoon resident of Jackson Ward in downtown Richmond, Virginia.

He was an architect by profession, and his designs were similar to those of Robert Stern, his mentor, but he surpassed even Mr. Stern in the art of utilizing every foot of space. A kitchen designed by Liam Wilton was a kitchen built to hold everything, while leaving countertops and window ledges free of clutter.

Liam's studio was on Brook Road, a mere three blocks from his house. Liam liked walking to work, and he liked observing, from his large picture window, the handsome brick triangle of land, that fronted his building and sported an imposing and rare southern live oak tree at its center.

The tree, scarcely a hundred years old, was forever green, rarely shed acorns, and offered a huge canopy of shade in the heat of summer, a protective umbrella of warmth in the dead of winter, and shelter from rain all year long.

Liam greatly admired the live oak; Jackson Ward residents boasted of the live oak, and visitors to downtown Richmond marveled at the majestic presence of such God-given living bounty in the midst of a building and traffic-laden metropolis.

But the tree was coming down. The mayor's plans for the renovation of Jackson Ward required its destruction, and the Richmond City Council had unanimously voted to approve the mayor's plans. Plenty of voices had been raised to protest killing the tree, petitions had been signed, an online PLEASE SAVE ME fund had been heartily pledged, letters to the editor had been published, posters had been carried up and down Broad Street for weeks on end—and still --- the tree remained slated for destruction.

The Jackson Ward Brotherhood of raccoons, squirrels, and possums was furious. That tree was their main transportation to rooftops that led to their nests and families and to many of the food sources they frequented. Not to mention that it housed birds, bees, and an infinite variety of insect life, and it offered temporary respite for monarch butterflies and coveys of migratory ducks and geese flying south for the winter season.

The Jackson Ward Wildlife Rotary Club called an emergency meeting. Lila Gleason Possum, guest speaker and President of the Jackson Ward Wildlife Women's Club, listened intently to every comment.

"Call in the governor and the secretary of natural resources. Humans are responsive to this kind of stuff," Bentley Bloodhound suggested.

"Not if money's involved," someone in the audience retorted, and someone else guffawed and emitted a low whistle of approval.

"Humans are the lowest where money's involved," Gordon Owl, former longtime city registrar concurred. "Why they'll devour their young if money's involved," he hooted, and the audience roared with laughter.

"This is no laughing matter. I've seen this destruction many times," former city council member Brightly Dunne Raccoon growled. "Whole parks and acres of forest stripped bare to make way for condos and parking lots. Entire wildlife families uprooted or killed outright and, in the Amazon and throughout South America, remote species of birds and wildlife rendered virtually extinct. Why, in Scotland"—he hesitated—"I wouldn't care to tell this if there were a roomful of ladies listening," he acknowledged, and nodded toward the podium to highlight Lila Gleason Possum's presence. "Pardon me, Lila, this is harsh," he continued, "but it's a matter of public record that in Scotland, during late spring and early summer, men, women, and children, armed with heavy sticks and wooden clubs, search for vixen dens, and then club to death the baby kits hidden inside them."

Lila Possum's eyelids shuddered closed, and she cleared her throat. "Gordon Owl is knowing and wise," she acknowledged to the attentively listening membership, "when it comes to human behavior and political clout, and Gordon honors and upholds the traditional procedures—debating the morality of issues—writing letters of protest, signing petitions, door-to-door contact with city residents—but what is needed here and now is a resistance that makes it clear to the mayor and the city council that the live oak is not to be destroyed."

And then she explained to the Rotary Club boys what her club had in mind.

The Rotary Club members, many of whom had wives and girlfriends who were members of the Women's Wildlife Association, listened.

A vote was called for and taken—Lila Possum's plan was resolutely endorsed, and a course of action was charted.

The resistance was to begin at once.

When Mayor T. Vulture Smith walked to his mailbox to get the morning paper, he discovered that the wooden stake to which his mailbox was affixed had been unevenly sawn in half and the newspaper shredded into confetti. "Blasted neighborhood vandals," he ranted. "This is why no one wants to live in downtown Richmond." He stalked back to the house. "Clarice," he hollered, "call the Times-Dispatch and tell them I need a paper, stat."

Clarice came downstairs a few minutes later. "The phone is dead," she informed her husband.

"What do you mean, dead?"

"I mean dead," she replied.

"Try the one in the den," he suggested.

"I tried them all, and they're all dead," she retorted.

"What the hell's going on this morning?" the mayor sputtered and strode outside to check the telephone wires from his house to the telephone pole. They looked okay to him, but they were too high up to say for sure. He walked next door and saw the morning paper lying on his neighbor's front porch. He was just about to nab it when the door opened and out slithered George Lipscomb Copperhead.

"Morning, Mayor Smith," George hissed affably, "What might I do for you?"

"George, is your phone working?"

"Well, my wife was doing her usual venomous chatting on it when I came out for the paper," George replied, "So I'd say the answer is yes."

Mayor Smith went back to his house, showered and shaved, ate a fast breakfast, kissed Clarice goodbye, and promised he'd have his secretary call Bell Atlantic and get the phones working ASAP. He slid behind the wheel of his Buick and did a quick double take. The entire windshield of his car was covered with paint. He looked more closely and realized that it wasn't paint. It was tar mixed with feathers, and on the windshield was inscribed "Kill no living thing," and on the rearview mirror was inscribed "First do no harm." And on the rear window was painted "Save the Tree!"

"What the hell?" he shrieked and shook a claw in outrage. "Somebody's going to find his teenage turkey tail in a sling for this tomfoolery." He got the garden hose and sprayed the windshield mightily, but it was impossible to wash off, and he ended up using several ice scrapers, two of which cracked. Then he got back into his car, turned on the motor and took off. He hadn't gotten more than three houses down when he realized that the Buick was riding on rims. He got out of the car and peered at the tires. Two of them were totally flat—with hundreds of irregular punctures—as if someone had taken a screwdriver to them or—he looked more carefully—or gone at them with tiny irregular saws. Chunks of tire torn away like—like nothing he'd seen before—like Hannibal Lector feasting on rubber.

He turned off the motor, walked back to the Lipscombs' house and asked to use their phone so he could call a cab.

The meeting was held in private—the Mayor, the Falcon SWAT, and the Richmond City Council. No secretaries, no reporters, and at the mayor's house, rather than City Hall.

"We need to get to the bottom of this," the mayor stated, and the council members, several of whom had been subjected to acts of petty vandalism, nodded agreement. The Richmond Falcon SWAT had been brought in, and the mayor and his council had waited for the culprits to be rounded up and booked. But a week had passed, the attacks had escalated, and no one had gotten caught and no one had gotten booked. There were no clues, no suspects, and no informants.

"I've a mind to fire the lot of you," Mayor Smith threatened. "Somebody's at the bottom of this, and I want to know who."

"There's nothing, I tell you," Chief Investigator Swanson Falcon told the mayor. "No prints, no clues, no witnesses, and no response to the one-thousand-dollar reward for information."

"Listen to me, buddy," the mayor expostulated, "this has gone on long enough. Get some plainclothes rats on the case, get whatever you need, but get to the bottom of this."

"We've had detectives and patrol crows on the lookout, Mr. Mayor, for nights on end, and not one of my men has seen or heard anything. I'm not sure God Almighty could figure this one out," Chief Swanson retorted.

Mayor Smith was a deacon of his church, and he bristled at the reference to God Almighty.

"I'll replace the lot of you with CIA bald eagles," he warned the SWAT. "You have one week to come up with the culprits." He held up a claw. "One lousy week, damn it!" he shouted. "Mea culpa, mea culpa, mea culpa," he quickly intoned and struck his breast three times for having cursed.

"One blasted week," he reiterated and strutted from the room, leaving the bewildered city council and the SWAT to figure out what next.

Mayor Smith had just finished lunch when his secretary buzzed him.

"Hairy Sweet Pea is here to see you," she told him, "and he says it's urgent."

"Show him in," Mayor Smith told her, and cleared his desk of sandwich crumbs.

Hairy Sweet Pea came in and sat down at the desk. He was a burly, clean-shaven city rat, and his three-piece khaki suit, worn with a handsome forest green and crimson striped regimental tie with a perfect Windsor knot, was impeccably tailored. He was known throughout Richmond as the mayor's henchman.

"This came this morning," he said and handed Mayor Smith a thick manila envelope.

The Mayor opened the envelope. It was a petition to save the live oak. There were 6,744 signatures, and below the signatures there was a circle the size of a silver dollar filled with tiny footprints. "Where did you get this?" the mayor demanded.

"It was in my mailbox," Hairy replied. "It doesn't have any postal service markings, so I assume it was hand-delivered."

"What's in the circle?" the mayor asked.

"Honeybee prints," Hairy replied.

"Honeybees are not money bees, Hairy." The mayor bristled. "Hell and damnation, man, we're talking about a multimillion-dollar plaza in the heart of Jackson Ward. Robbule Coyote has been buying up Broad Street buildings for more than fifteen years, and he wants the Brook Road triangle at the heart of his multimillion-dollar shopping spree. He wants to turn it into a plaza with a gargantuan bronze statue of himself where that blasted tree has taken up residence. It'll be the most dramatic thing that's happened to Jackson Ward since Maggie Walker opened her money-lending business."

"I know all of that, Mr. Mayor. I know all of that and more. I know that you don't go against nature, when nature determines otherwise. The critters that inhabit that tree and use it for refuge and transportation have formed a coalition. Did you see the cartoon on the editorial page of the Richmond Times-Dispatch yesterday? The Richmond City Council, in full military regalia, on horseback, brandishing chainsaws, and you, on a huge evilly grinning stump grinder, and the nobly drawn live oak, with its majestic limbs chained behind its imposing trunk, and hundreds of adorably rendered little critters hanging on for dear life from the doomed tree's twisted and manacled branches. The Times-Dispatch switchboard has been lit up like a Christmas tree with irate calls from irate readers. There's plenty of opposition to killing that tree."

"It's not the first time we've had to deal with opposition, Hairy," the mayor retorted. He leaned back into his chair and eyeballed Hairy with skepticism. "Are you suggesting that a passel of signatures and the imprinted endorsement of powerless honeybees on a petition and an afternoon of phone calls to the Times-Dispatch from overwrought tree huggers are more powerful than the mayor, the city council, and the moneyed movers and shakers who run this city?"

"If they go against us, they could be," Hairy said quietly. "They've already destroyed tires, severed telephone wires, painted 'You shall not side with the mighty against the powerless' and 'What you do to the least of them, you do to Me' on billboards and City Hall windows—not to mention that every telephone pole east of Belvidere and Broad has a poster with "Thou Shall Not Kill" nailed to it. And now—" Hairy shook his head in escalating dismay—"now there are rumors about disruption of the entire sewer system in downtown Richmond. These opponents mean business, Mr. Mayor, and they keep abreast of everything you say and do. Take a look out your window."

Mayor Smith swiveled his chair around. There were dozens of honeybees, with their antennae pressed to the plate-glass window. "What the hell do bees have to do with that live oak?"

"There are hives in that live oak, Mr. Mayor, many hives. Bees listen with their antennae. Those bees have their antennae pressed to the glass. I suspect they're eavesdropping."

The mayor swiveled his chair back around and stared at Hairy. "Where are you going with this, Hairy?"

"I'm toying with the notion that you might consider not cutting down the live oak; maybe construct Robbule's plaza somewhere else—perhaps Abner Clay Park. That location will work out just as well."

"I have no intention of bending my will to a bleeding-heart, tree-worshipping passel of petition signers. I'll have the entire lot of tar-and-feather slinging birds picked off, one by one, by the Richmond SWAT, and the hives are going to come down with that overgrown live oak." He buzzed his secretary. "Rhoda, get in here and bring that can of Raid with you. My windowsill's swarming with bees."

But when Rhoda came in with the Raid, the bees were gone.

Mayor Smith and Clarice were just sitting down to dinner when the telephone rang. There was a sewer leak underground, and City Hall was flooded with the worst smelling water imaginable. Every time the repairmen got one leak stopped, another spurt erupted. By midnight, all of Broad, from Tenth Street to Belvidere Street, was ankle deep in dark brown water and reeked. Jackson Ward sewer rats were manning the side streets, where Jackson Ward residents huddled inside their houses and apartments, bathroom deodorizer-saturated handkerchiefs held to their nostrils.

And then it started to rain, only not just rain—heavy rain followed by strong gusts of wind and hail the size of mothballs. Windows were blown in, storefronts were battered, and critters trying to reach the safety of their houses were knocked unconscious by the hail and rushed to MCV and—when the MCV emergency room was filled to overflowing—to Retreat Hospital, St. Mary's Hospital, Henrico Doctor's Hospital, and then to hastily set-up emergency shelters.

It was two in the morning before the wind died down, the hail stopped, and the leaks were curtailed.

But Jackson Ward and downtown Broad Street were a mess.

The following afternoon, while watering his tomato plants, the mayor was engulfed by a swarm of buzzing bees and badly stung. He was rushed by ambulance to Richmond Memorial Hospital and placed on a respirator. His underbelly and breast had to be completely de-feathered, and he was injected with cortisone and given emergency treatment to slow down his rapidly escalating heartbeat.

It was all over the five o'clock news.

It took a week for Mayor Smith's beak, neck, underbelly, breast, and wings to return to their normal size, and when Mayor Smith walked to the podium to announce the change of plans for the plaza site, his beak and neck were still lumpy, but he looked a lot better than he had the week before.

His fearsome claws barely shook when he read the proposal the Richmond City Council had unanimously endorsed concerning the Mayor's radical change of plans for the Maggie Walker Plaza that was to be situated on the triangle of land at Brook Road and Broad Street.

The revised plan, which included the live oak's staying put but being cut back to allow for easy foot traffic was, the Mayor told the astonished reporters, what he had always personally envisioned, and it was why he had recently signed the online petition to save the live oak.

The newly appointed Maggie Walker Plaza Commission was to be headed by Harry Sweet Pea Rat. Lila Gleason Possum was second in command. Julia Honeybee was to be secretary. Cornelius Mosby Crow was to be treasurer, and the newly appointed architect for the site was to be Liam Wilton Raccoon.

"No architect in the world," the Mayor asserted, "could execute a more comprehensive blueprint for that small triangle of land than Liam Raccoon."

"And," he added, "it was and remains a matter of record that no one loved oak trees more than Maggie Walker and that, by having that splendid live oak remain in situ to grace the Maggie Walker Plaza, the City of Richmond continues its aesthetic and ecological endorsement of Maggie Walker's legacy."

The Mayor's announcement was followed by a resounding wave of applause, and after the press conference was ended, coffee, tea, sandwiches, and tray after tray of cookies, made by the Jackson Ward Women's Wildlife Association, were joyfully served and joyously consumed

"Men argue. Nature acts."

Voltaire

BRIDGE IN THE AFTERNOON

For the Blue Bayou and GreenAcres Regulars -

Tandy Josef Kady Sidley O BoTexas Egret Michkey Avataric Zoltan DurangoMom Nonie Hodgie Khankhalifzal JoeySquirrel mnt dharvey crazybutfun Sassy ZeldaRidesAgain Victor YoungGoodTiger Tarzan Smitty RenoRaines Houcheboy Fishnet Gedova Colo Sugo Sledrider Herscheka MMCragdoll FariamJuane mildredbenjamin Sylvie Paden'sGranny NakedFirebug ArmyBeatsNavy CaptDLT Zeroweightflyman Pablo DuelsDavis hoopsnake snavesplay MKC coffee-2hot Jermish GRL cowboyJoe Raisinply elmay hero

> "Men rise and fall like winter wheat,
> but these names live on."
> —Homer, *The Iliad*

Jake Egret was Hampton born and bred. His father was an egret of Armenian descent and owned a chain of drugstores, and his mother was a snowy white pelican, descended from a long line of French ne'er-do-well aristocrats. She was beautiful and haughty, and she had married Jake's father for money rather than for love. She gave him five daughters before finally producing a male heir. When Jake was hatched, she asked if it was a boy.

"Yes," Dr. Suggs replied, "you finally have a son."

"Good," she said, "now tie the tubes."

Jake's mother died when Jake was a toddler. She had flown to Nice to nurse her mother, who was gravely ill with avian cholera, and both she and Jake's grandmother succumbed to the insidious disease.

Jake and his sisters were cared for by a hastily-employed, gruff, and uncompromising German hedgehog housekeeper named Hilda, and by their carousing and generally absent father, in a modest bungalow, situated in a thickset topmost branch of a magnolia tree located on a property aptly named "Pasture Point." Two of Jake's sisters, the second and the fourth, had died before Jake was born—one of "bird fever" at six months of age and the other, when she was two, of injuries sustained from an interstate collision into the windshield of a Mack truck.

The three remaining daughters married and moved away not long after their mother's death and, shortly thereafter, Hilda ran off with a widowed ferret major she had met at the officers' club at Fort Monroe, Virginia.

Jake continued to live at home with his father, but their relationship was not congenial. His father had a quick and brutal temper. He would cuff Jake violently with the back of his claws over the slightest annoyance and, although he had plenty of income, he let the bungalow fall into disrepair and spent most of his ready cash on women and backroom poker games.

Six months after Hilda ran off, Jake's father was stabbed in the parking lot of Eat Dirt Cheap at Fuller's in downtown Phoebus. He died from septicemia ten days after the stabbing occurred. Bernie, Jake's father's only sibling, was arrested and interrogated but not indicted. The sordid particulars that lay behind the stabbing were said to involve Bernie's wife. The incident made headlines in the Daily Press, and the ensuing gossip spread like wildfire. The scandal rapidly demolished the family's standing in the community, and Jake's sisters and their husbands, who had flown in for their father's sparsely attended funeral, left town immediately following the reading of the will.

Jake mourned neither his father's death nor his sisters' absence. His father had left a modest amount of money to each of his three daughters, but the bulk of his estate was left to Jake. He inherited the magnolia tree bungalow, a truckload of blue-chip stocks and the drugstores, which he quickly sold and converted into U.S. treasury bonds. He fixed up the bungalow to suit his taste, hired a muskrat named Toby to maintain it, and bought an elegant oceanfront condo in Palm Beach. He shared none of his inheritance with his sisters because, when his mother died and left her fine French antiques and jewels and furs to her daughters, they had not shared so little as a pinky ring with him, despite the fact that her will had been written before Jake was born.

Turnabout, he reckoned, was fair play.

※❀〜❀※

Jake suspected that he was, at heart, a misogynist. He was not fond of his sisters. His eldest sister was methodically grasping. His middle sister was self-centered and wild. And his youngest sister was a sycophantic tattle-tale. Nor had he been close to his mother. She had catered to him because he was the requisite male heir, but they had not bonded as mother and son and, after her death, his caretaking—relegated to his three muddled sisters and Hilda—had been indifferent and unaffectionate. He became an outsider in a household of cold and secretive women, and his understanding of the female sex remained vague and wary.

But he was a handsome fellow—tall, with long sturdy legs, his mother's capacious yellowy orange pelican bill and a pristine overcoat of snowy white feathers. His eyes were keen and well set in a shapely head, topped with an imposing cowlick.

And—now that he was prosperous—many a female eyed him longingly, and many a mama eyed him approvingly as a potential son-in-law—but to no avail. Time rolled on, and Jake remained a resolute bachelor.

※❀〜❀※

Jake's great passion was for cards. He had played the numberless types of solitaire endlessly as a child and had learned Canasta from his paternal grandmother. She taught him the game with even-natured patience, and he endured the merciless routine of watching her count her many points while judiciously praising the meager points he had managed to garner. After months of losing every round, Jake finally caught on to the knack of melding. Impassive of expression, he would shrewdly assemble his hand, delay until the last possible moment, and then casually lay down his cards. His grandmother was never able to best him at Canasta again. And so she gave up on Canasta and taught him bridge.

Jake took to bridge the way a duck takes to water. He loved the precision of counting his points, assessing his hand, and exchanging cue bids that made it possible for him to know exactly what his partner had and for him to convey to his partner exactly what he had. He relished doubling his opponents and then setting them mightily, and he especially loved making grand slams and bidding transfers that netted stolen bids from less adept players.

His favorite bridge partner, Madeline Marie Crane, was a cute and sassy schoolteacher from Minnesota. They had met at a popular stopover en route to Palm Beach for the winter season, and Jake had noted and admired her stylishly-coiffed feathers and shapely dangling legs in flight.

Madeline Marie played rummy and canasta with the regulars who frequented the stopover, but she didn't know a thing about bridge. It had taken many lessons for Jake to teach her the intricacies of the game but, with time and patience, they began to bid and play flawless bridge as partners. They seldom lost a rubber, and when they did lose, it was because they had been dealt inferior cards.

Madeline Marie was married to a Hungarian stork named Laszlo—a diamond broker Palm Beach habitué who never flew north for the summer, spoke flawless English with a thick accent, sported a carefully trimmed moustache, and donned custom-fitted silk vests, replete with a Patek Philippe minute repeater and a gem-studded watch fob attached to a heavy gold chain. He was assertive and moneyed, loved cricket and soccer, despised all card games, chain-smoked Havana cheroots, and paced incessantly.

It was rumored that Laszlo maintained an exotic and buxom pink flamingo mistress in Vero Beach. But Madeline Marie didn't seem to know or to care if she did know. She had her summers in Minnesota, her classes at Sacre Coeur, an exclusive Palm Beach academy where she taught medieval history, and she had bridge in the afternoon with Jake Egret.

Madeline Marie was the first to acquire a computer. They had begun using them at Sacre Coeur, and Madeline Marie quickly became computer proficient.

Within weeks, she discovered Pogo, an online gaming website that made it possible for creatures living in different states, different countries, different time zones, to play bridge at all hours of the day and night. She told Jake, who was ecstatic. "That means we can play online from anywhere and at any time," he said jubilantly.

Jake bought two iMac computers, installed one in the Hampton bungalow and the other in the Palm Beach condo, and he and Madeline Marie began to play Pogo Bridge online. They started in a beginner's room that was named Blue Bayou and played rated games until they had both reached the intermediate level and then they played unrated games. They played together every afternoon, but never at night or on the weekends because Laszlo wanted his wife entirely to himself in the evenings and during the weekends.

And so, Jake Egret began playing evening and weekend online bridge with other partners. He played with coffee2hot, who was clever and witty and rarely over bid his hand but had a temper. He played with Anita Beagle, who was good but took too long, and with Revolving Rita, who was jovial and played okay but left the table at the drop of a hat. She would abruptly announce, "I'm sorry, partner, but I've got to go," and leave smack in the middle of a hand. He played with Otto Osprey, who was inflexible and moody and not nearly as good a player as he proclaimed himself to be, and he played with Reno Raines, who always kept track of the cards, and knew when to double and when not to double but took offense easily.

Occasionally, during the weekdays, a part-cottontail rabbit named Mildred Benjamin would sit down at Jake and Madeline Marie's table. She was a decent player, and she was sweet natured and well mannered. She never seemed to mind losing to Jake and Madeline Marie. She also didn't seem to mind playing with a robot partner, which happened fairly often, because most of the Pogo members hated to lose, and Jake and Madeline Marie were known to be formidable opponents, whereas Mildred Benjamin had a low rating.

But Jake had observed Mildred's game, and he could see that she had the potential to be an excellent player. What he most liked was that she played a quick hand. Slow players drove him up the wall. And he liked that Mildred Benjamin never left before the rubber was completed.

He added her to his friends list and read through her profile. It didn't reveal much.

"Standard American bridge—strong two bids, weak three bids—no transfers—five card majors—thirteen points to open."

She hadn't listed her favorite movies or types of music or her hobbies.

But she had listed a favorite quote:

*Anything will give up its secrets
if you love it enough.*

The quote intrigued Jake. Why had Mildred Benjamin included it in an otherwise bland profile? He harbored no secrets and he wasn't interested in finding out anyone else's secrets, unless they involved mastery at the bridge table.

He scrolled back up and scrutinized Mildred Benjamin's photograph.

She was wearing a tartan-plaid jumper and a white, piped-in-navy, cap-sleeved blouse with a Peter Pan collar, also piped in navy. The straps of her jumper were crisscrossed, and one of the straps had slid beyond her shoulder and onto her furry little forearm, in the crook of which a baby squirrel was peacefully ensconced.

Her feet, long and slim, sported a pair of black patent leather Mary Jane shoes and navy-piped white socks.

Youthful, Jake thought; innocent, he thought; and totally entranced with the baby squirrel upon which her gaze was fastened.

One afternoon in November, while Jake and Madeline Marie were playing their second rubber, Laszlo came home from the office early. He told Madeline Marie to turn off the computer and call the doctor because he was feeling faint and had an alarming pain just below his left wing.

Madeline Marie excused herself from the bridge table, and Jake was ready to leave, too, when Mildred Benjamin came in and took the seat across from him. They finished out the rubber and were beginning a third rubber when Jake asked her if she ever played bridge during the weekends. "No," she replied, "I only play during the weekdays. I do wildlife rehabilitation on the weekends."

"Too much chatting," Otto Osprey complained.

"Sorry, Otto," Jake replied, and Mildred Benjamin apologized, too. They completed and won the rubber, Otto and his partner vacated the table, and Mildred Benjamin ventured that she was glad she had gotten a chance to play with Jake rather than against him.

Jake thought for a moment. "Well, would you be willing to play partners with me on a regular basis, during the weekdays?"

"Oh yes," she replied, "but I can only play after one o'clock. I'm on weekday morning duty at the infirmary in my warren from six till noon, and I live with my mother. We spend the evenings together watching our favorite TV shows and playing dominoes and cribbage until bedtime. I go to bed rather early," she confessed.

They settled tentatively on Monday through Friday afternoons from two until four.

Jake then asked Madeline Marie, who had taken a leave of absence from Sacre Coeur, if they could switch from playing bridge in the afternoon to playing bridge in the morning.

Madeline Marie said that playing in the morning would actually suit her better because Laszlo, who liked to sleep in late, had suffered a mild heart attack and would be at home in the afternoons until he recovered.

And so Jake Egret and Mildred Benjamin Bunny began playing afternoon bridge together. Jake, an egret of few words, accepted without complaint or criticism her unorthodox bids and the paucity of her knowledge of bridge conventions. In time he expanded her skills. He taught her Gerber, Michaels, and Stayman—when and how to bid transfers, the rule of eleven in no-trump hands, and when, with two five-card majors, to bid spades first and when to bid hearts first.

Mildred Benjamin was always grateful, always eager to learn, but not always on top of her game. Occasionally Jake grew impatient with her, but he always apologized afterwards, and she always justified his outbursts, always expressed her amazement that he, a genius at the bridge table, was willing to take her on as a regular partner.

Oh, she was an endearing little creature, that Mildred Benjamin! And she learned quickly. But if she had a sick bunny that concerned her, or if one of her patients was badly injured or unable to eat, or if one or both of her paws were bandaged because of bites and scratches from a rehab possum or squirrel and her typing came out jumbled and incoherent, Jake would know that Mildred Benjamin was not going to play up to par that day, and he would pull at his cowlick in impotent frustration and wish that she would learn to play with the sanguine precision of a Madeline Marie Crane.

In time, Madeline Marie's husband became well enough to return to his office, and Madeline Marie informed Jake that she was going to be teaching morning classes again and that she was now ready to resume playing partners with him in the afternoon.

"What about Mildred Benjamin?" Jake asked.

"What about her?" Madeline Marie retorted. "She can just play at our table with a partner other than you," she added indifferently.

But the idea of Mildred Benjamin playing bridge against him, instead of with him, stuck in Jake Egret's craw. He lay awake in his Palm Beach condo all night, weighing the pros and cons of having Mildred Benjamin as an opponent, and he finally decided that his playing against her was not going to happen because . . . because it wouldn't work out and couldn't work out because . . . because it would just be a muddle of—of—well, of something he could not even begin to know how to put into words.

Mildred Benjamin was gracious when Jake told her why they could no longer play as partners in the afternoon. She thanked him for helping her to improve her game and said that she would never forget him and that she would sorely miss bridge in the afternoon with him.

But her bids that afternoon were totally off the wall, and her playing that afternoon was totally off the wall, and they lost seven rubbers in a row. Mildred Benjamin apologized after each incorrect bid—each botched finesse—each failure to return his opening lead—and Jake replied "no problem" each time and did not address or chastise her errors or ask if she'd been bitten by a rehab squirrel or if she'd had a bad morning at the infirmary or what in the world had happened to the fine level of mastery she had achieved since they began playing as partners.

They played their final round in virtual silence and, after the rubber was completed, Mildred Benjamin typed out a misspelled goodbye and a jumbled promise that she would stop in and say hello to him and Madeline Marie soon.

The days passed slowly and became weeks. The weeks passed slowly and became months. Madeline Marie's bridge remained impeccable, but she was starting to seriously get on Jake's nerves. He kept a watchful eye out for Mildred Benjamin, but she clearly wasn't playing bridge in the afternoon, and she hadn't stopped in to say hello as she had promised she would, and Jake began to keenly mourn her absence.

She finally came in, many months down the road. It was after midnight, and Jake's partner was Otto Osprey, and their opponents were robots.

She thumped out a shy greeting to Jake, ventured that she hoped he and Otto were winning against the "tin men," and then, quick as only a cottontail can be, she hopped out of the room, and out of the Blue Bayou lobby, and was gone.

Jake felt a stab of longing that lingered and intensified. He told Otto he was going to bed and left the bridge table abruptly, pulled up his Pogo friends list, clicked onto Mildred Benjamin's name, scrutinized her photograph, and scrolled down and read and reread the intriguing quotation she had included in her brief profile.

He then scrolled back onto her picture and, when he gazed upon the slipped-down, plaid jumper strap, and then upon the blissful baby squirrel nestled in the crook of her furry little arm, bittersweet comprehension flooded his mind and rapidly beating heart, and Jake Egret finally acknowledged what it was that he had been unable to put into words.

"If I had not been a crow," said he,
"I would have married her myself,
notwithstanding that I am already engaged."
—Hans Christian Andersen,
"The Snow Queen"

THE GOOD THE BAD AND THE HIDEOUS

For Henry

"*I detest the man who speaks forth one thing and hides in his heart another.*"
—Homer, ***The Iliad***

Nancy was a Marymount School born and reared chicken. She never knew the hen that laid her because she had been carried, still in shell, to the Science Lab at Marymount and left to hatch beneath a heat bulb in a small aquarium.

Nancy broke free of her shell on Easter Sunday. The lab was empty, the boarders had gone home for spring break, the nuns were in chapel, and there were no siblings and no clucking mother hen to greet her. So this is it, she thought. This is the moment I've been awaiting. She edged out of and beyond her shell and peeped plaintively. Her cries echoed beyond the aquarium and bounced off the walls of the sterile lab. Nothing and no one responded, and so she lay wearily down on the impersonal straw and descended into the stupor of sleep.

When the nuns returned from Easter service and discovered her, they took endless turns holding her, kissing her pale orange beak and marveling at the tininess of her body and the shininess of her piercing black eyes. They named her Nancy and provided her with a small bowl of water and grub worms and other delicacies from the convent's garden. And two days later the boarders returned from holiday and took turns holding her and kissing her tiny beak.

One boarder in particular, Sarah Archer, fell in love with Nancy. She would sit with Nancy in the afternoons, until sunset, and then cover the aquarium with a Lanz granny nightgown and, before she went to sleep, she would set her radio alarm for 6:00 A.M. and, the minute it went off, she would rush down to the lab and slip Nancy into the pocket of her navy uniform skirt. She took Nancy everywhere—to classes, to the dining room for meals, to study hall, to chapel for morning prayers, and then back to the aquarium at dusk.

Nancy liked attending classes with Sarah. She learned how to add and subtract—how to multiply and divide—how to punctuate a letter—why Napoleon was both a hero and a villain—how gravity held the planets in place—and why Earth was the most hospitable of all the planets. But her favorite class was literature. She marveled at the poetry of Edgar Allan Poe—the silken, sad, uncertain rustling of each purple curtain thrilled her, filled her with fantastic terror never felt before—terror akin to the isolable memory of awakening to life in the sterile glass aquarium into which she'd been born. Why do I exist—she wondered ---Why do I press forward to endure and achieve?—Why am I apprehensive?—Where and how do I fit in?

On April Fools' Day, Sarah Archer's roommate was expelled for setting fire, at five in the morning, to a trashcan in the science lab, which then set off the fire alarm. Everyone was hurried out of the building, but Sarah rushed back to the lab and quickly gathered Nancy into the folds of her Viyella bathrobe. She never returned Nancy to the lab after that. Where Sarah went, Nancy went.

At sunset, Sarah would wash Nancy in the bathroom sink and dry her with a soft towel. And then she would put Nancy in a laundry basket lined with pieces of cotton bunting and cover the basket with a square of sheet.

At dawn, when the first rays of sunlight shone through the slatted blinds of Sarah's bedroom window, Nancy would awaken to the sound of Sarah's rhythmic breathing. She would peep until Sarah reached for and gathered Nancy's tremulous body into the warmth of the eiderdown quilt that had belonged to Sarah's grandmother, and then Sarah and Nancy would nestle together until the warning bell for morning chapel rang.

When the semester was completed, Sarah Archer's father sent his chauffeur to drive Sarah home. Sarah's belongings were placed in the boot of the Bentley, and Sarah settled into the rear seat of the commodious automobile, with Nancy alongside her. The trip from Richmond to Poughkeepsie, New York, was a long one, and they were both sound asleep when the car pulled into the Douglas fir-lined driveway of the Archer estate.

The Archer estate consisted of an old farmhouse, a greenhouse, a smokehouse, a gazebo, a barn, and a chicken coop that was ruled by a hen named Bridget.

Bridget was gangly and bow-legged, with darting black eyes and a harsh cackle. Her two offspring, Monty and Betsy, were replicas of their mom—notwithstanding that Monty was a rooster.

Bridget disliked Nancy. At the core of her dislike lay envy of Nancy's relationship with Sarah Archer, who was now enrolled as a freshman at Vassar. But Bridget determined that her antipathy for Nancy was for good reasons. Nancy put on airs, Bridget cautioned the coop members. She continued to disregard the coop's routine. She was just plain spoiled rotten.

Sarah took Nancy to classes daily and returned her to the coop before sunset. They no longer shared sleeping quarters because Sarah's mother would not permit Sarah to bring "that hen" into the house, so Nancy slept in the coop with the other hens and baby chicks. But Bridget saw to it that Nancy was regarded as an interloper.

A few of the roosting hens and baby chicks continued to gather around Nancy when she returned from her daily trek to Vassar with Sarah, and they would listen attentively to what Nancy had to say. She explained to the baby chicks that the planet on which they were living revolved around the mighty sun, and that the stars which glowed at night were little suns, and that the moon determined the ebb and flow of the seven seas, and that all rivers and lakes returned to the sea from whence all life had begun. But what she most loved was to share, with the more mature hens, the beauty of the written word—

> the bittersweet yearning of Shelley
> ("We look before and after,
> And pine for what is not . . .
> Our sweetest songs are
> those that tell of saddest thought");
> the spiritual wisdom of Coleridge
> ("He prayeth best, who loveth best
> all things both great and small");
> the psychological acuity of Shakespeare
> ("Such men as he be never at heart's ease
> Whiles they behold a greater than themselves,
> And therefore are they very dangerous").

After a while, Nancy began writing poetry. Sarah thought one of her poems, entitled "Rain," was really good. She submitted it to The New Yorker for publication, and they accepted it.

Sarah was proud of Nancy, and so were many of her feathered friends at the Archer coop, but Bridget loathed Nancy's success and disparaged Nancy's writing by never acknowledging it, never reading it, and cautioning the coop to have nothing more to do with Nancy because, although she pretended to be oh-so-proper, she was, at heart, a Philistine. She was, Bridget coaxed them in honeyed tones, and had always been a bad egg.

More of the coop members, in the wake of Bridget's pronouncements, became wary of Nancy, and Nancy realized that she might soon need to make other housing arrangements.

The move came after a disagreement concerning a praying mantis. Nancy had just returned from classes with Sarah and was heading to the Archer garden for a meal of tender corn when she saw several chicks pecking the mantis. Its shell had been badly punctured, and one of its wings was partly torn away.

"Stop pecking at it," Nancy admonished the baby chicks.

"Finish it off," Bridget instructed the chicks. "We kill them," she informed Nancy acridly. "We kill them because they're hideous, and they're not one of us." Her eyes flashed hatred, and Nancy saw that Bridget's loathing of her and of the mantis was deep and relentless and had nothing to do with moral rectitude. She quickly snatched up the mantis and carried it to the cornfield. She wasn't sure it would survive the night. But it did survive the night, and when morning came, Nancy gently washed the sticky ooze from its wounded shell and gave it water and tiny bits of food, which it grasped with its pincers and slowly consumed. Within a week, the mantis was well enough to tell her that his name was Franklin and that he was a born-and-bred New Yorker and, when he thanked Nancy for saving his life, tiny tears spilled from his eyes.

Nancy was shunned by most of the coop members after that episode, and Franklin was astute enough to understand, after his traumatic foray into the Archer coop, that he must never venture there again.

And so Franklin built a house of twigs and cornhusks, held together with loam, beneath one of the sturdy lower branches of an old butternut tree situated at the farthest boundary of the Archer estate.

The house was just large enough to accommodate himself and Nancy but, in time, with the royalties from a published volume of Nancy's poetry, they were able to add a small library, a storage unit for blankets and linens, and a kitchen with running water and a tiny fireplace.

Occasionally a few renegade chicks from the Archer coop would drop in for an afternoon cup of tea and freshly baked cornbread with butter and jam, and sometimes they would stay for supper. Franklin was always a gracious host, and the chicks, apprehensive of him at first, began to see him in a new light. He was, they conceded, a mantis of distinction.

Sarah Archer got pregnant that summer and gave birth to a son. The father was the husband of a relative, and Sarah gave the child up for adoption. It was the year of the muumuu, and she concealed her pregnancy by wearing voluminous and gaily-patterned muumuus. She spent the last trimester with her paternal grandmother and maiden aunt in her grandmother's brownstone in Greenwich Village.

After the baby was born, Sarah returned to Vassar. Eight months, later she became pregnant again, this time by one of her professors. She again gave the child—a daughter with a shock of white blonde hair and piercing blue eyes—up for adoption. The same couple who adopted her son took her daughter and, when Sarah was waiting to sign the adoption papers, her lawyer left his office to take a personal call, and Sarah quickly looked through the manila file on his desk and saw the names and address of the adoptive parents. She wrote the information on her left arm, before her lawyer returned. She was sweating so heavily she was afraid the ink would wash off, but it didn't, and when she returned to her grandmother's brownstone, she copied the information down in her diary.

Sarah's father died the following year, and Sarah's mother sold the house in Poughkeepsie and moved to Boca Grande. The new owners kept the coop and chickens, updated the henhouse, and installed a handsome black rooster to maintain law and order. Monty moved to Capri and made good money as a bartender at The

Blue Grotto Bistro. Betsy fell in love with a well-heeled lawyer from a prominent Ayam Cemani family, but he married a buxom debutante from one of the neighboring estates, and Betsy stayed on with her mother.

Sarah—peacefully ensconced with her paternal grandmother and maiden aunt—asked if Nancy might come to live with them. Her grandmother said yes.

And so, the following week, Nancy moved in, and a week after that, Franklin flew in.

❧

Sarah was cautious of Franklin. He had an uncanny way of turning his head and peering at her. She'd never seen an insect do that. He followed Nancy everywhere and settled atop Nancy's tail feathers when she strutted the brownstone's spacious courtyard. Mosquitoes and mites avoided Nancy like the plague because of Franklin.

Nancy and Franklin drank from the same water bowl, pecked the ground side by side and, at dusk, when Nancy retired to the small shed behind the courtyard, Franklin retired with her.

❧

Sarah fell in love with a Jewish sculptor named Hershel Drucker. Sarah's mother, a devout Catholic, forbade the marriage and declined to give her daughter a wedding, but Sarah's grandmother adored Hershel, and so Sarah and Hershel were married at City Hall and lived with Sarah's grandmother and maiden aunt while Hershel completed his master's degree at Columbia.

A year later, Hershel accepted a teaching position at Richmond Professional Institute. He and Sarah moved to Richmond and lived in a tiny third-floor apartment on West Franklin Street. They stayed with Sarah's grandmother and maiden aunt during the holidays, for spring break, and during the summer.

Nancy would pick up Sarah's scent before Hershel's Volvo station wagon came to a stop in front of the brownstone, and she would peep and run in tight circles until Sarah came out to the courtyard to see her. Franklin would follow shyly behind, but at a watchful distance.

Sarah finally lost her fear of Franklin. She grew fond of him, and Hershel thought Franklin a prince of a fellow. Franklin took to flying onto his shoulder and staying perched there whenever Hershel wandered into the courtyard.

"I wish they knew how to play bridge," Hershel told Sarah. "It would make for an interesting table."

Nancy and Franklin grew older together. Nancy, who had been vegetarian since the formation of her relationship with Franklin, was now plump, wrinkled, and slow of strut, and Franklin's antennae had grayed. His beautiful green shell and wings sported tiny age cracks, but his health and state of mind remained strong.

He and Nancy were inseparable.

Who can explain love? It either is, or it isn't.

Franklin was at Nancy's side the morning she died. She had awakened in pain—pain, she gasped, as if a thousand boulders were pressing down on her chest.

She smiled tenderly at Franklin, caressed his shell with her beak and gazed into his prominent eyes for a long while. "I love you, little one," she told him.

Her vision began to falter. "It grows dim," she murmured, "to hold the light."

"Oh!" she whispered.

"How beautiful!" she whispered.

And then she closed her eyes and off she went in search of the great perhaps.

The gardener buried Nancy that evening in Sarah's antique and intricately carved mahogany treasure box, with Sarah's grandmother and maiden aunt and Franklin in attendance. The sky was filled with stars, and the moon was full. It sent silver to the silver beech tree beneath which Nancy's body had been laid to rest.

Franklin, aching with loss, flew to the gardener's shoulder. "Hey, little fella," the gardener said to him. "I'm sorry you've lost your friend."

Franklin gazed mournfully at the silver beech. "Will you help me?" he pleaded silently.

And so, the silver-laden tree revealed itself to Franklin: its radiant aura—the pulsating electrons in the outer shells of its leaves—the vibrant life force that emanated from its trunk and limbs. He saw as he had never seen, and he knew as he had once known but forgotten.

Franklin flew from the gardener's shoulder and up—up—up until he reached the topmost branch of the silver beech tree. His body was suffused with moonlight and he saw that the moon's rim had turned yellow—the exact yellow of Nancy's underbelly—and Franklin came to know that nothing ever dies—it merely steps beyond the form that has contained it.

Franklin stepped beyond his form three days later. The gardener discovered him on Nancy's grave, head to one side, pincers folded, as if in prayer. He informed Sarah's grandmother that Franklin had died. Mrs. Archer handed him Sarah's grandfather's beaten copper cigar box and asked him to put Franklin in the box and bury him under the silver beech tree, next to Nancy, which he did.

"Goodbye and Godspeed, little fella," he murmured, and headed back to the house, cap in hand, to tell Mrs. Archer that he had done as she asked.

"The courtyard won't be the same without them two," he said quietly.

"No," Mrs. Archer replied, "it won't be the same."

Sarah and Hershel drove to New York that weekend.

Hershel recited Kaddish for Nancy and Franklin, and Sarah placed a plaque, engraved with their names, above the graves. Below their names was inscribed a quote from Goethe:

"We are shaped and fashioned by what we love."

And then Sarah told Hershel about the son and daughter she had given up for adoption. Hershel asked her why she had given them up, and Sarah said that her mother had insisted that she do so. Hershel observed her for a long moment.

His face registered sorrowful comprehension and, when he gathered Sarah into his arms, she began to cry.

"I want to know the mind of God.
The rest are details."
Albert Einstein

"I give you truth in the pleasant disguise of illusion"
Tennessee Williams, *The Glass Menagerie*

THERE'S NO BUSINESS LIKE SHOW BUSINESS

For Ernest and Emil

"With Major Lawrence, mercy is a passion. With me, it is merely good manners. You must decide which motive is more reliable."
—***Lawrence of Arabia***

May and June flew from Florida to Hampton, Virginia, every spring and knew the travel route perfectly. They went from Clearwater to Savannah, from Savannah to Charleston, from Charleston to Myrtle Beach, and from Myrtle Beach to Kitty Hawk or Nags Head, depending on the wind. From there they went to Virginia Beach, and from there to Hampton, Virginia. They spent spring, summer, and most of autumn in Hampton. The property where they stayed was on the Hampton River, and it was named Pasture Point.

They always made it to Pasture Point in time for Dr. and Mrs. Jamerson's annual Easter egg hunt and supper party. It began at sundown, just before the mallards were ready to retire for the evening. The guests would spill onto the broad pie-shaped span of lawn. The children would take handfuls of cracked corn to feed the sizeable gathering of mallards, and the adults would take handfuls of whole corn to toss high into the air for the seagulls circling overhead—who were not really interested—seagulls had their own particularities of delicacy, and corn was no treat to them—but they reveled in the lively crowd and performed stunning gull spins and daring gull cartwheels that dotted the twilight horizon.

Oh, yes! For May and June, Easter at Pasture Point was the most festive part of coming home!

May had returned to the Clearwater apartment following an afternoon of last-minute trip shopping to find

June lying on the divan, left wing over her forehead. "I hope you're not having an attack of vapors," May stated cryptically. "Are you packed?"

June moaned.

"Well, are you?"

June sat up and handed May the letter she had tucked under the cushion of the divan. "Read it," she said.

It was from the Peabody Hotel. The hotel manager and staff were thrilled and eagerly anticipating the arrival of Miss May Jamerson and Miss June Jamerson. Their accommodations were ready, and the troupe of resident ducks was abuzz with excitement over their arrival.

May folded her wings against her chest. "I'm not going, June. I told you I wasn't, and I'm not."

"It's a wonderful opportunity," June honked. "Why not? We can certainly try it for a season, and if we don't like it, we can quit."

"Is that what you think, silly girl? One doesn't just walk out of a place like the Peabody. Once we sign on, we're theirs. We won't even be permitted to step outside, apart from a brief daily walk around the roof garden. And you can't fly off from the roof garden, because the first thing the Peabody does after the contract has been signed is to clip the wings and tail feathers of its performers to prevent their flying anywhere. Trust me, June, you'll hate the Peabody after a month. No freedom, everything is rote, and the folks who come to see the Peabody Duck Parade are not worth the monotony of riding the elevators up and down, swimming in a small chlorinated lobby pool all day long, and choking down the occasional stale morsel of breakfast brioche, thrown by guests who blatantly ignore the "please do not feed the ducks" signs posted everywhere. Not to mention that the Peabody ducks are not integrated. We'd be the only mallards in a troupe of washed-out honkies. No, thank you."

"Well, I'm going," June retorted.

"What about Dr. and Mrs. Jamerson and the children?"

"They'll understand. We can send them a postcard from the Peabody. They're all caught up in their own lives. They're not in charge of us. They're not even our real parents."

"What an ingrate you are!" May remonstrated. "Why, the Jamerson family took us in when we were orphans. They let us paddle about in their largest and deepest bathtub, installed a huge rock in the center of it so we could rest when we wearied of paddling. And then, when we got older, they took us outside and watched over us during our first treks to and from the river, protected us from predators as we came and went, and then opened the kitchen door for us and watched with delight as we waddled through the kitchen and butler's pantry—into the laundry room and then to our cozy nesting box for a night of peaceful sleep."

May shook a scolding wing at June. And then she reminded June of how, when the weather began to chill, Mrs. Jamerson would pack a hobo bag with cracked corn and dried berries and grains, and of how she and Dr. Jamerson and the children would oversee their departure and bid them Godspeed during their long flight south for the winter.

"They've cared for us and watched over us for years," May said, "and we've always had the freedom to choose for ourselves when to come and go."

"That's what you're really honking about, May," June said archly. "You can't stand not being the decision maker. The idea of signing a contract and following someone else's routines and rules scares you to death. Well, you just do as you please. I want to be in show business."

"Don't do this, June. You'll be a token mallard at the Peabody. And you'll be unhappy," May said.

But June's mind was made up

And so the sisters parted ways.

※ ※

Dr. and Mrs. Jamerson always began their preparations for the annual Easter egg hunt and supper well in advance of the event. Quail eggs were hidden inside the house and Easter baskets for the children—filled with chocolate bunnies, jelly beans, sugar-frosted lemon and orange slices—were tied with bows and hidden under bushes, in the lowest limbs of trees, in the rose garden, in the boxwood maze, in flowerbeds—everywhere little searching eyes could spy them.

Mrs. Jamerson was in charge of supper, and her menu was always the same—roast leg of lamb, deviled eggs, Chesapeake Bay crab salad, baked Smithfield ham, corn pudding, a medley of fresh lettuces and garden vegetables, penne pasta with peas and gorgonzola cheese, and, for dessert, Lady Baltimore cake, four layers high—filled with pecans, raisins, coconut and grated orange rind and frosted with an almond butter cream icing. And there were brownies, chunky chocolate chip cookies, and baked caramel custard with fresh strawberries and whipped cream.

The children would search for the Easter baskets while the men drank their whiskey and the ladies sipped their sherry, and there would be whoops of excitement each time a basket was found. Then came supper. And then the indoor egg hunt—tiny quail eggs, hard as the dickens to find—cleverly disguised as a part of the figurines on which they rested, tucked into the intricate gold-leaf frames of paintings, nestled inside barely opened tulips, balanced atop lampshade finials, secreted in bookcases, inkwells, silver bowls, crystal bowls, porcelain bowls, next to sofa legs, table legs, behind photographs, on mantels, lintels and windowsills.

Everyone would search and search, but Mrs. Jamerson would always find three or four undiscovered eggs the next morning, and the housekeeper would happen upon one or two more really well-camouflaged eggs, many days down the road.

The evening culminated with dessert—a difficult choice for grownups and children alike, and there were many declarations of, "I'm going to try a little bite of every dessert on this table!"

But-always-always-and-always—for May and June—the most thrilling part of the Easter egg hunt was seeing the littlest boys and girls stream outside—their eyes wild with excitement as the circling multitude of honking ducks gobbled the cracked corn from their upturned little palms.

May was forlorn over her sister's absence, and the Jamerson family was heavy-hearted, too. Their eyes had searched the lawn when May toddled up to the kitchen door and knocked on the glass panes with her strong bill.

"But where is June?" Mrs. Jamerson asked. It pained her to see May standing on the brick stoop alone and, when the sun had set and May waddled into the laundry room and climbed dejectedly into the nesting box without her sister, Dr. Jamerson was unable to console his wife and children.

"She'll be along in a while," he told them reassuringly. "June will be back. She's just been delayed. Don't fret, my dears. June will come home soon."

But he was worried, too. May could see it in his eyes and hear it in his voice.

It was Holy Thursday, three days before Easter Sunday, and May was heading back to the house after her daily swim in the river when she heard a strange rustling in the boxwood maze. At first she thought it was a cat, and she was debating whether to make a fast waddle to the house or take wing to the safety of the river, when she heard a tiny honk that sounded like her name being called. She hesitated on one flat foot, and then she heard it again—a soft and very weak May—May—May. She hurried over and peered under the leafy bush. She could not believe her eyes. It was June, her beloved baby sister June, but it was a June she had never seen before. She was thin, she had circles under her eyes, there was a long scratch on the left side of her bill, her feet were bruised and blistered and her feathers—well—her feathers were a disaster! Her wing and tail feathers were unevenly cut, and most of them had been thickly painted an ugly grayish-white. She looked unattractive and unwell—but worst of all, she looked desolate.

"Oh, my goodness," May exclaimed and burst into tears. "You look like death warmed over," she sobbed. "What's happened to you?"

June spilled out the story in weary honks. She had made it to the Peabody, and everyone had been thrilled to have her—overjoyed to have her. But things had turned quickly sour. She had been the belle of the ball, the hit of the duck parade. Until the troupe grew tired of her—tired of the exclamations over her richly colored Mallard feathers—her exotic beauty—her uniqueness—her charm, and—most particularly—her endless stories of her trips from Florida to Hampton and of the fascinating creatures she had met during her travels.

One night, after she had fallen asleep, the white ducks snatched her from her nesting box, held her down, and painted her finely colored feathers with whiteout they had purloined from an office secretary's desk drawer. When June tried to get away, they scratched and bit her, stomped her webbed feet until they were bruised and blistered. "At first, they loved me," she moaned, "but then they hated me. Oh, May, envy is surely a terrible sin, and those honkies were full of it."

May started to say that she had warned June not to go to the Peabody, but her heart was filled with compassion for her sister, and so she reassured June that Dr. Jamerson would take care of her injuries, and that time would heal every scratch and bruise, and that her clipped feathers would grow out, and the ugly typewriter whiteout would grow faint and finally disappear.

"But how in the world did you manage to get home?" she asked June.

"I was hiding out on the roof garden," June confessed to May. "The Peabody didn't want me in their parade anymore, and the hotel manager didn't want me in the lobby anymore because I looked so awful, so I hung out on the roof garden during the day and slept behind the air conditioners at night, and finally I wrote out and tied a 'Hampton, Virginia,' hitchhiking sign around my neck and stood on the balcony ledge of the roof garden and prayed for someone to take notice of me. I had just about given up hope when an older gentleman named Jake Egret landed on the roof. His keen eyes had spotted the sign around my neck and so he swooped down, listened to my tale of woe, and then scooped me into his huge pelican bill and flew me here. He was on his way back to Pasture Point when he spied me, May. Imagine the good fortune of that! He flies to Florida every winter, but he lives here at Pasture Point the rest of the year, just like we do. He has a bungalow in the huge magnolia tree closest to the river and he's the kindest creature I've ever known. He fed me at every stopover, made sure I had a comfortable place to sleep, and when anyone poked fun at my appearance, he warned them to shut their bills before he took a hard peck at them. Oh, that Jake Egret was the answer to my prayers! And,"- June's eyes sparkled with excitement, "Guess what? Jake is engaged, and we're both invited to the wedding. His bride-to-be is from Pawley's Island, and her name is Mildred, but he calls her 'Millie'."

May tried to pinpoint which egret Jake might be, but there were many egrets that routinely flew in and out of Pasture Point. She settled her sister beneath a secure branch of boxwood and then she waddled over and stood beneath the huge magnolia tree closest to the river and honked an emotional 'thank you' to Jake Egret for his caretaking of her baby sister. And then she added that she greatly looked forward to meeting him and his bride to be. And then she returned to June's side and kept watch over her in the boxwood maze.

The Jamerson family was overjoyed to find May and June waiting side by side at the kitchen door that afternoon. The children fussed over June, and Mrs. Jamerson cooed over June, and Dr. Jamerson filled the laundry room sink with warm water laced with Dawn detergent and washed much of the whiteout from her feathers. He assured her that her tail feathers and wing feathers would be quite long enough to take her South for the winter season, and that the scratch on her bill wouldn't leave a scar, and that the bruises on her webbed feet would disappear completely with time.

And, that night, when May and June went into their nesting box, they nestled so closely that the two of them appeared to be one duck.

June wouldn't be persuaded to venture onto the lawn for the festivities. She was ashamed of her feathers and embarrassed by the scratch on her bill and the unsightly bruises on her webbed feet, and it still hurt to waddle anywhere because the Peabody ducks had torn away part of one claw. So, Dr. Jamerson carried June upstairs, and she stood on the broad sill of the upstairs sitting room bay window and watched the hoopla with vicarious delight and a sense of bittersweet accomplishment for having tried and survived her disastrous foray into show business. She would never do anything quite so foolish again—but it would be quite a valuable lesson to share with her children and grandchildren and quite a story to tell at the stopovers during the return flight to Florida.

Later that evening, after the last plate of dessert had been eaten and the last of the guests had bidden a fond farewell, Mrs. Jamerson brought May and June an Easter basket, tied with a pink silk bow, and filled with quartered Muscat grapes, multi-grain birdseed, broken pecan pieces, thinly sliced vegetables and, for dessert, fresh strawberries and morsels of filling from the Lady Baltimore cake.

A pair of small, lace-trimmed damask napkins was tucked into the pink and green Easter grass. May and June exclaimed over the precision of their needlework, and then neatly folded them and put them aside. The hand-stitched beauties would, they agreed, make a perfect wedding present for Jake and Millie.

"Leave them alone and they'll come home
Wagging their tails behind them"
"Little Bo Peep"

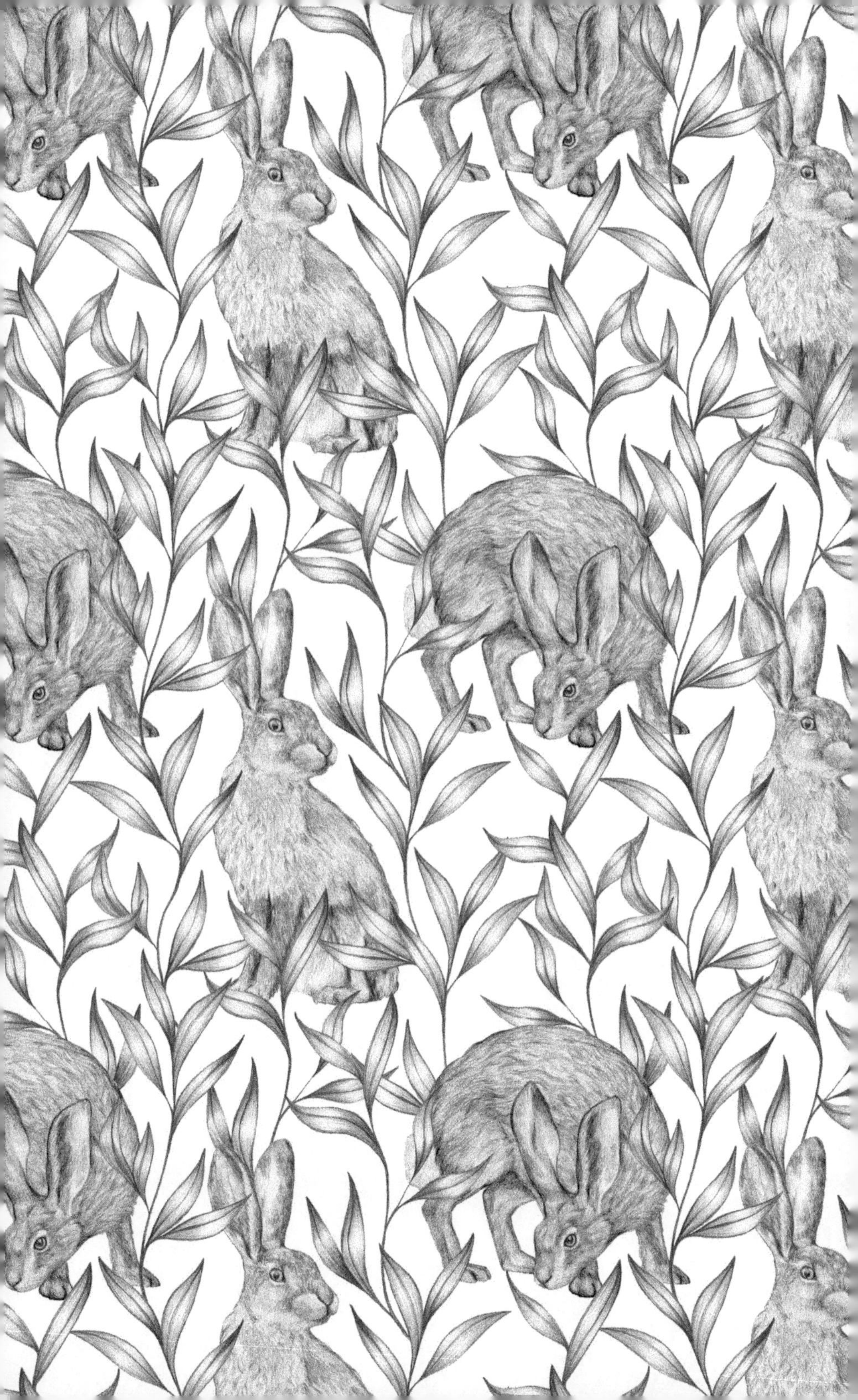

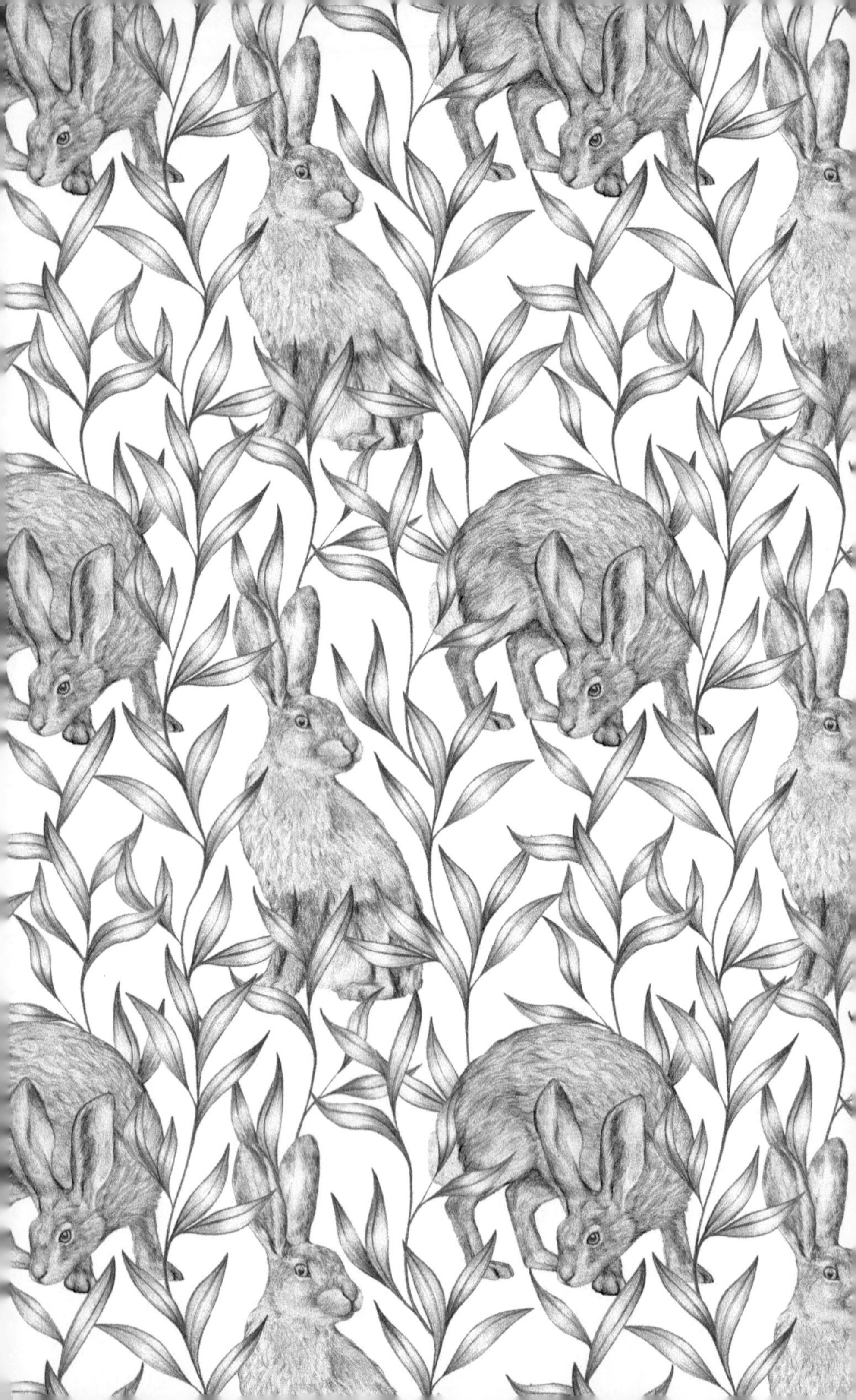

Mariah Robinson loves to wrap a story around a good aphorism. She began collecting them when she was ten and has clothbound and handwritten volumes of memorable quotations tucked away on shelves, in closets, and atop a large, oak, library writing desk. Mariah's first novel, *Love and Other Illusions*, was nominated in 2012 by the Library of Virginia for best in Literary Fiction. *Sister Sorrow, Sister Joy*, her second work of fiction, has also been nominated for best in Literary Fiction in 2019. She is currently writing a children's book entitled *Joseph Bottomley*. She lives in Richmond, Virginia.